T0365356

Muffin & Mamma

Make Challah

story by Louise Siegel
art by Valery Herman

To order additional copies of this book, contact:
Xlibris
1-888-795-4274
www.Xlibris.com
Orders@Xlibris.com

# Muffin and Mamma Make Challah

Story by Louise Siegel
Illustrations by Valery Herman

Mama is an older lady but she still has lots of energy. She works out at a fitness center and grows beautiful flowers.

Muffin is a young cat and has lots of energy too. She races around the house and climbs to the very top of her cat tree. Sometimes Mama thinks that Muffin has too much energy!

On Friday mornings Mama gets out her extra large mixing bowl and Muffin knows it's her job to help Mama make challah.

Mama gets out all the ingredients she will need: flour, sugar, yeast, warm water, eggs, plus measuring cups and a clean towel.

Muffin helps Mama remember to put on an apron so she won't get flour on her clothes.

Muffin has her own apron!

Mama carefully measures eight cups of flour into the bowl

and then adds the sugar,

yeast

and warm water.

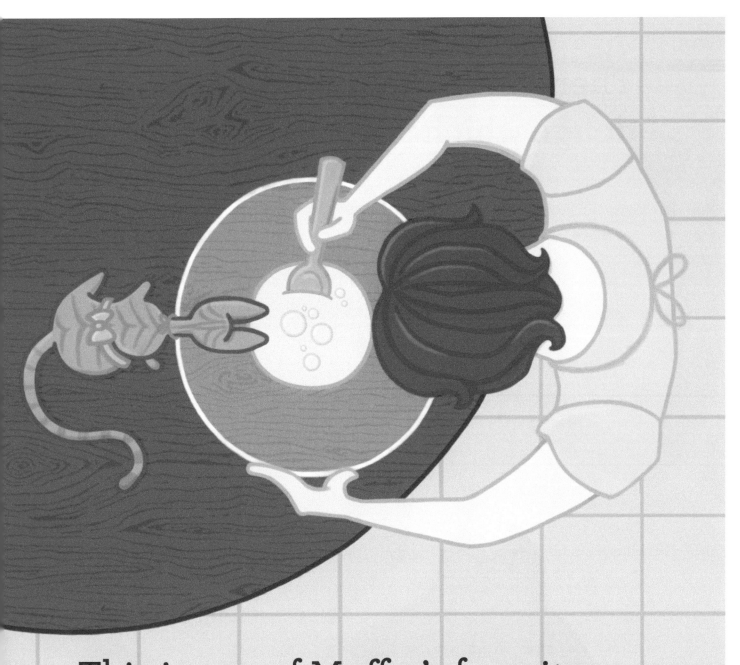

This is one of Muffin's favorite times to watch the yeast and sugar begin to bubble together as if the challah is starting to come alive!

Then mama begins to knead the dough which takes a lot of energy.

Mama had to learn how to knead dough but Muffin already knew how since cats do it by instinct. Muffin practices on her scratching post.

When the dough feels just right, Mama puts a clean towel over the bowl and puts it in a warm oven to let the dough rise. Muffin likes to look in the oven window.

When the timer goes off, Mama takes out the bowl and lifts off the towel. The dough has risen to the top of the bowl. Both Mama and Muffin give the dough a little pat to see if it feels just right.

Then Mama punches down the dough and separates it into three sections. She rolls each section into a long snake. Muffin measures to make sure they are all the same length.

Then Mama starts to braid the dough—

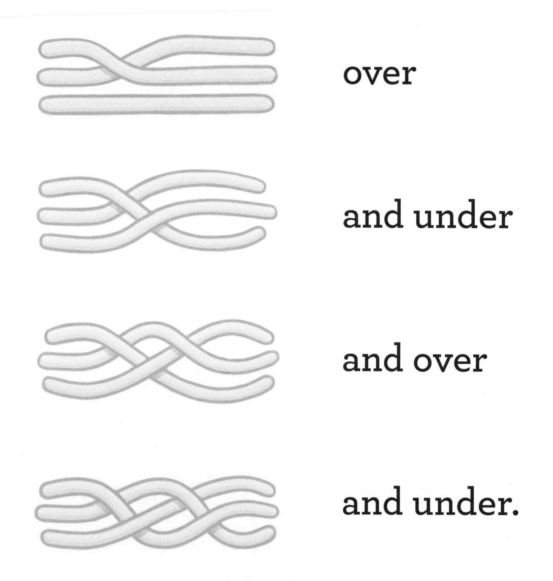

over

and under

and over

and under.

Muffin helps Mama keep track.

Then Mama puts the dough back in the oven to let it rise again. Muffin thinks this is a good time to take a nap!

Finally, the dough is almost ready to bake. Just one more step. Mama brushes egg yoke on top to make the dough shiny.

Muffin likes the leftover egg yoke as a treat!

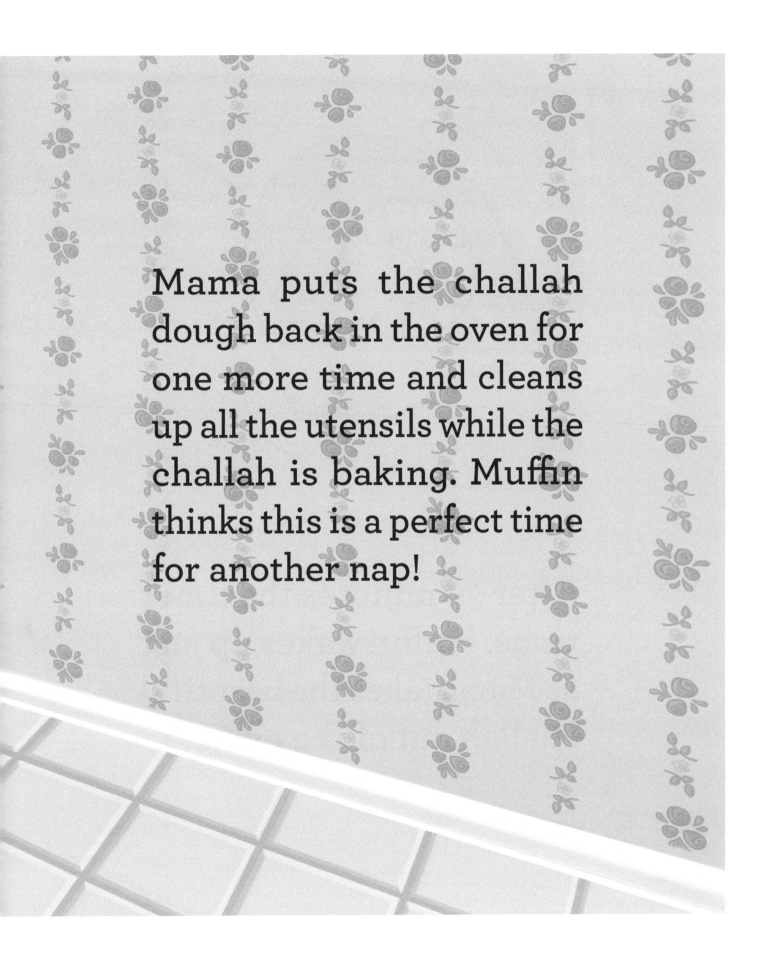

Mama puts the challah dough back in the oven for one more time and cleans up all the utensils while the challah is baking. Muffin thinks this is a perfect time for another nap!

After 30 minutes the timer
rings. Muffin wakes up just
as Mama takes the beautiful
challah out of the oven.

On Friday night Mama's family and friends come for Shabbat dinner. Muffin's friends come too!

Mama's challah has the
place of honor on the table.